Solomon Walker Young

Legends and Lyrics

Solomon Walker Young

Legends and Lyrics

ISBN/EAN: 9783744786751

Printed in Europe, USA, Canada, Australia, Japan

Cover: Foto ©Andreas Hilbeck / pixelio.de

More available books at **www.hansebooks.com**

BY

SOLOMON WALKER YOUNG

" What is writ, is writ,
' Would it were worthier"
— CHILDE HAROLD

BOSTON:
THE WRITER PUBLISHING COMPANY
1890

CONTENTS.

LEGENDS AND LYRICS.

LEGENDS AND LYRICS.

PROEM.

IT is a valley fair and green ;
  The shadows dark of maples tall
And orchards, glimmering in the sheen,
  On garden sleep and cottage wall.

On morning's breath is fragrance sweet
  Of pink and rose ; in shady nook,
Like footfalls light of gentle feet,
  Comes merry sound of dancing brook.

Morn's happy voices lull the ear :
  The sparrow's chirp, the hum of bees,
The robin's note ; anon I hear
  The wind's low murmur in the trees.

But more than charms of sound or sight
  Are visions, by fond memory traced,
That wrap the scene, like halos bright,
  Which envious Time has not effaced.

This vale, the circling hills, wood-crowned,
  With shapes of wakened memory teem ;
There is a spell in sight and sound,
  Recalling vanished scene and dream.

The joys that brightened bygone days,
  Fond hope's inspiring song of cheer,
Life's cares and griefs, its darksome ways,
  Pleasures and pains, — they all are here.

But some, now dim to memory,
  Black clouds of care almost conceal;
And others few, seen mistily,
  These simple pages will reveal.

Will any heed such brief review
  Of common scenes, where manhood wrought
Or childhood played? or hear anew
  The strain that banished sadder thought?

Perhaps for some who love to hear
  Quaint legends of a vanished age,
To whom calm rural scenes are dear
  And Nature's clear and ample page,

For them this rustic strain may bear,
  If they scorn not the poet's lay,
Some beams of pleasure, brightening care,
  Or solace for a weary day.

But if my lays no answering chord
  Shall wake in all the restless throng,
Then shall they be their own reward ;
  The dearest meed of song is song.

SONGS OF LABOR.

I.

A GARDEN wherein all was fair :
    Soft light and shadow's play ;
Smooth lawns that knew no want of care,
Green slopes, bright flowers, and statues there,
    And silver fountain-spray.

Wide canopies of leaves o'erhead,
    Affording grateful shade,
Where linden, oak, and maple spread
Brown arms o'er shrub-lined paths, that led
    To arbor fair or glade.

A bridge here spanned a narrow lake,
   Its arch with granite laid;
A boat-house, and, of faultless make,
A tiny boat the light waves brake
   And childish hands obeyed.

Along the shore was many a seat,
   Inviting to repose;
There, under branches, weary feet
Sought rest within the cool retreat;
   There hearts forgot their woes.

Beyond, a stream, sail-whitened, lay;
   Tall spires and city walls;
On thousand roofs the sunbeams play,
On busy streets, on walls of gray,
   On parks, and courts, and halls;

On rural haunts and villages
   By river-shore or mere ;
On homes that nestled under trees,
Fair mansions, humble cottages,
   With fruit-bent orchards near.

O'erhead was heard, in ceaseless flow.
   The happy birds' gay song ;
The hum of labor from below.
Or echoing bell-stroke, fast or slow.
   Where busy myriads throng.

And far away, beyond the reach
   Of fertile meadow lands,
Glimmered a line of sea-worn beach.
Whence rose at times the faint-heard speech
   Of waves by white sea sands.

But while I gazed with raptured eye
  Vanished the lovely scene :
And then I saw. in fancy, rise
A landscape in a darker guise.
  For landscape fair and green.

On all the hills and valleys spread
  The gloom of endless wood :
No trace of man but such as led
A life befitting scenes so dread —
  The beasts were scarce more rude.

Around the walks and fountains gone,
  The flowers and fruit-hung tree ;
The wolf prowled o'er the thick-grown lawn :
Beyond, a landscape wild and wan :
  Deep woods shut out the sea.

Like this, I thought, our pleasant land
  Was once, in grove and field, —
A strange, wild scene, a waste of strand
And wilderness, — till labor's hand
  Its wonders had revealed.

While I the vision pondered o'er,
  And then, with happier thought,
Recalled the view of vale and shore,
I clearly saw, as ne'er before.
  The work by labor wrought.

II.

On meadows green the sunlight fell,
  The gloom had passed away:
And now from breezy lawn and dell,
From spring-fed plain and echoing swell,
  Low voices seemed to say:

" O lover of the pleasant glade
   And valleys bright and green.
  Forget not him whose toil has made
   So fair the peaceful scene :

" Who felled the forest, cleared the mead,
   With verdure clothed the hill :
  Who broke the glebe and sowed the seed
   Whose harvest ripens still.

" 'Tis labor's skilful hand has wrought
   The myriad forms of art ;
  It bars the stream, and rears the cot,
   The mansion, mill, and mart.

"With all things fair adorns your home :
   It spreads the snowy sail,
  And speeds the ship through wave and foam,
   The engine on the rail.

" It delves the mine and frames the gin,
    Gives all most prized and rare,
  And searches sea and stream to win
    For you all treasures there.

" It writes your books ; its busy pen
    Reveals all known to man,
  And bids the ages pass again
    Since changeful time began.

" And since so much you surely owe
    To labor's friendly aid,
  Remember that the debt by no
    Unkindness may be paid.

" Lest selfishness from duty swerve,
    Guard well the fleeting hours,
  And strive your fellow-man to serve ;
    For others use your powers.

" Nor with the toiler be it said
    You fear his task to share;
'Tis idle hearts the future dread.
    And yield to vain despair.

" Labor gives rest from vexing care,
    And grief and passion's strife :
It gives new life ; the stagnant air
    With poison's breath grows rife.

" Disease, and poverty, and pain
    Wait on the idle throng ;
But working hand and working brain
    Together shall grow strong.

" Then honor give the toiler due,
    Whate'er his lot and state,
By whose strong arms your nation grew
    So mighty, free, and great."

THE CASTALIAN FOUNTAIN.

A BOVE the vale of Pleistus
　　This ancient fountain rose
At the foot of Mount Parnassus,
　　Fed by his wasting snows.

Near shone the towers of Delphi
　　And temple, where of old,
Amid three thousand statues,
　　Apollo stood in gold.

There maidens, dazed with incense, —
　　Their voice has long been dumb, —
Foretold the fate of battles
　　And weal or bale to come.

Castalia this temple
  With ceaseless flow supplied,
Mingled in many a sacred rite
  Its pure and sparkling tide.

Sang 'round the fount the Muses;
  'Tis said, for ages long,
Who drank of its pure waters
  Received the gift of song.

Gone is the ancient city,
  The temple is no more,
The statues other temples
  Adorn on foreign shore.

No longer roam the Muses
  On Phocis' famous mount;
No more they join in choral lay
  Around the sacred fount.

But yet its shining waters
   Still clearly, brightly flow,
As when the poet drank them,
   Three thousand years ago.

Not vain the ancient legend,
   For many a flowing rill
And many a sparkling fountain
   Inspires the poet still.

No more from heathen deities
   The bard shall aid obtain;
Apollo's lyre is silent;
   The siren's deathful strain,

The Muses' art, the fountain's spell, —
   They all have passed away;
But Nature's many voices still
   Inspire the poet's lay.

THE MINISTER AND HIS CRITIC.

ONE Sabbath, in a neighboring town,
　　Preached to a goodly audience
A worthy man,[1] of much renown
　　For wit and eloquence.

At noontide, 'round the open door
　　And wooden columns tall and white
That rise the little church before,
　　And glisten in the light,

The people tarry as they come,
　　Chatting, from vacant pew and aisle.
Many the sermon praise, but some
　　Condemn the preacher's " style."

At length spake one of unknown name,
  A man unlearned, but bold of speech :
" He's a good man, but hain't, I claim,
  Co-pacity to preach."

The " good man " to his rest has gone,
  But, 'mid the scenes where long he taught,
In grateful hearts he still lives on :
  His critic is forgot.

Thus ofttimes critics, who assail
  True merit with unsparing hand,
Condemn what their weak brains but fail
  To grasp or understand.

Some time have brightest names of earth
  Been tarnished by reproach and blame ;
The world at last has owned their worth ;
  Who now their critics name ?

THE FARMER'S WILL.

THERE was once an honest farmer,
  When and where it matters not;
Wide his fruitful fields and woodlands,
  Plenty blessed his ample cot.

Far from din and strife of cities,
  From their tumult and display,
Cared he little for their splendor,
  Restless crowds, or fashions gay.

Oft in summer you might see him
  Toiling in the clear, bright air,
Happy, while the sun looked kindly
  On his meadows rich and fair.
To his cheerful hearth in winter
  Friendship came and banished care.

When abroad he wore a "beaver"
　　Quite remarkable for size;
Down behind it touched his collar,
　　And in front it reached his eyes.

Vest of satin, "pants" of doeskin, —
　　Such our honored fathers wore, —
And his coat was of a pattern
　　Made some twenty years before.

In his rural home, contented,
　　Near his children, half a score, —
Oftentimes he wished the number
　　Were indeed as many more, —
Dwelt and thrived this honest farmer
　　Till his years of toil were o'er.

Then he called his children 'round him:
　　"I am feeble grown and old;

Rests in peace your sainted mother
   'Neath the churchyard's hallowed mould.
Soon 'twill be my lot to follow.
   All my lands, and stocks, and gold

" I bequeath to you, my children,
   And I only ask of you
What remains of this life's journey
   That you bear me safely through;

" That you give me food and shelter
   From the sun, and wind, and snows,
And forsake me not in sickness
   Nor life's troubles till its close."

All were overjoyed, these children,
   When their father's wish was known;
And they took his presents gladly,
   And they called his lands their own.

And they made a faithful promise,
  For his kindness they, in turn,
Would a home provide and living —
  Ne'er too old are we to learn !

Now, it chanced that with a daughter
  First his home the farmer made,
And arranged his few possessions
  As if long he would have staid.

For she was a favorite daughter,
  Who had been his joy and pride,
Whom he had indulged and petted ;
  Scarce a wish had he denied.

But her husband for their aged
  Father had but small regard ;
Whose old-fashioned ways displeased him,
  Or perhaps his heart was hard.

Growing weary of the burden
   Soon, he cross and sullen grew,
And he blamed his wife for doing
   What the brothers ought to do.

Such expense ! an imposition,
   He declared, it surely seemed.
'Twas enough to clothe the children.
   Thus he reasoned and he schemed,

Till the daughter to her father
   Hinted he would better fare
In " the nicer home of Johnnie ";
   So the farmer hastened there.

Scarcely in his new home settled,
   He was forced once more to change ;
" Small the cottage for so many."
   He began to think it strange.

William, who came next, was noted
   Most for indolence and rhyme,
And he looked as if he thought his
   Father came before 'twas time.

Then came Timothy, his brother,
   Prudent, miserly, and cold ;
What he had, believed in keeping,
   Nothing prized so much as gold.

So not long the farmer tarried.
   Thus, with sad and anxious thought,
Slighted, weary, poor, neglected,
   Peaceful home in vain he sought.

To a country teacher " boarding
   'Round " he well might be compared,
Or to some itinerant peddler,
   Though not half as well he fared.

Vexed, at length, and tired of travel,
    And a plan that seemed so nice,
Sought he now a friendly lawyer,
    Told him all, and asked advice.

" Get a trunk," replied the lawyer,
    " With a lock of curious make,
All so strong and oddly fashioned
    None can either pick or break.

" Gather pebbles by the lake-side,
    Or where cliffs of shelving slate,
Cleft by rain and frosts of winter,
    Scatter fragments small and great.

" Often to your room repairing,
    As concealed a precious store,
Make them rattle, rattle, rattle,
    As you count them o'er and o'er."

Thus the farmer did ; his children
   Heard him count his treasure o'er,
And they heard the rattle, rattle,
   Through the partly open door ;
Thought they heard the ring of silver
   And of gold, a secret store.

Now of all the place afforded
   Everywhere he had the best :
And whene'er he came his children
   Begged him tarry long and rest !

Best he had of food and clothing,
   Cosy rooms wherein to stay —
Counting oft his stony treasure
   When from curious eyes away.

More than all, in grief or sickness,
   Best of friends to care for him :

Ere his round was once completed
    Life's declining day grew dim.

When, at last, his life was ended,
    There was much of grief and tears,
And the trunk was not forgotten
    That had been a hope for years.

So they gathered, these fond children,
    Where they thought great wealth in store,
And they went away — some wiser,
    Though no richer than before.

Moral : Never pay the workman
    Till the promised work is done ;
And if you've a dozen children,
    Look out well for *number one.*

THE POET TALKS WITH ECHO.

ONE day a poet, strolling near
  A grove where Echo chanced to be,
Made some inquiries rather queer.
  When Echo heard him, saucily .
She mocked him, but — the little elf —
Garbled his words to please herself.

"Shall I," he asked, "with light romance
  And strain weak Folly most shall prize,
Seek to amuse dull Ignorance?
  Or for the scholar, keen and wise,
Now wake the harp, in accents late,
And, patient, his approval wait?"
Quoth Echo rather pertly: " *Wait!*"

Again the poet, half afraid,
   Asked : "Should my aim be to delight
My neighbor, or instruct and aid ?
   Plainly, hereafter shall I write
To please or benefit mankind ? "
But Echo, more to suit her mind,
Said : " *Please and benefit mankind.*"

Once more he questioned : " Shall I write
   For profit, gold, and pelf, rewards
To every witless, lucky wight
   Which Popularity affords ?
Or, like the honored bards of yore,
Seek rather to be rich in lore ? "
But Echo only answered : " *Lore !* "

" Shall I," the poet asked again,
   " Still frame the light and sportive lay ?
Or, in more solemn, earnest strain,

Some task more difficult essay,
That will surprise my poet brother,
That, haply, would o'ertask another ? "
Said Echo, laughing : *"Ask another !"*

" What," then he asked, " shall be my theme ?
    Pernicious war, despair, and woe ?
Some scene of Nature, lover's dream
    And rhapsody on cheeks that glow,
On eyes that sparkle, lips that don't " —
Quoth Echo, interrupting : *" Don't !"*

" What if the critic, carping, cross,
    Should all my careful work condemn,
By ridicule turn into dross
    The precious thought that seemed a gem ?
Fleeing from evils that surround him
To fall on others that confound him ? "
But Echo only said : *" Confound him !"*

" Echo, I see thou art a friend ;

    Thou knowest well my humble name

And where my thought and labor tend;

    Shall I then strive for greater fame,

Renew the youthful zeal near spent,

Or with small honor be content ? "

And Echo answered :   " *Be content !* "

A NOVEMBER SCENE.

GONE are the spring's delightful hours,
    June brightness, summer heats are past;
Seared leaves lie thick in autumn bowers,
    Nude branches tremble in the blast.

There is no lay of singing bird,
    No whisper from the ice-bound rill;
Only the piping winds are heard,
    And sighing branches on the hill.

Alone, of all the meadow's pride,
    The drooping glass-blade seeks the sun,
Still green, though faded all beside,
    And flowers have perished, every one.

But under frost and ice we know
   Still summer life and warmth delay :
In Nature's bosom, veiled in snow,
   Still beats the merry heart of May.

"Tis thus the piercing winds of woe
   The soul's deep currents may not chill :
The cares of age, like winter's snow,
   May vanish, and leave gladness still.

And though the brow is silvered o'er,
   Old eyes grow dim, and limbs are cold,
The heart is merry as of yore :
   The soul, that dies not, grows not old.

THE SUNCOOK.

A WINDING stream, unknown to fame,
   The Suncook bears its ancient name[2]
  'The Indian gave before
  One white man trod its shore.

Fair stream ! now imaging in light
The autumn woodlands, clear and bright ;
  Whose glistening shower falls
  O'er frowning granite walls ;

Whose morning mists brown meadows hide
And shorn fields sloping to its side ;
  By hill, and vale, and isle
  Its placid waters smile.

From wood-veiled fount on mountain side,
Far down the long, bright vale, the tide
 Past mart, and lawn, and lea
 Winds slowly to the sea.

Past din of loom, and rushing wheel,
And ringing bell its waters steal ;
 O'er falls, where dash and roar
 Its waves on rocky shore ;

Past glades that bask in noonday beams,
Where ploughmen urge their drowsy teams ;
 Past homesteads in the shade
 Of maple colonnade ;

Along the marge, with flowers lined,
Rude paths, bough-shaded, curve and wind ;
 Aster and hazel bloom,
 Still cheering autumn's gloom ;

Tall golden rods by sheltering hedge ;
And peering o'er the water's edge,
  In one secluded place,
  The cardinal flower's face.

Years have not changed thee, river fair,
Though changed thy shores and all they bear:
  The old has passed away,
  The new grown old and gray.

Thy margin green, in sun and shade,
Was boyhood's playground; there once strayed
  The fisher with his rod,
  These banks the hunter trod.

Charmed with the scene and blissful days,
'Twas here I tried my first rude lays
  That mocked in measured rhyme
  The waves' melodious chime.

I view, in fancy, sheltered nook,
Green boughs that arched the warbling brook,
    Brown paths that led through shade
    Or flower-scented glade;

The steep banks flushed with morning's ray,
Light shadows in the stream. at play,
    The bridge of golden light
    That spanned the waters bright;

And youthful faces, long unseen,
Of those who trod the slopes of green,
    Who slumber by thy side,
    Or in far homes abide.

These images, and many more
That wake old memories o'er and o'er,
    With darker visions pass
    Within thy magic glass.

Of ages past few tokens tell :
Here fickle fame did never dwell ;
   Few vestiges to trace [8]
   Left of a former race.

But common sights of earth and sky
Now greet us : yet as years glide by,
   With each returning year
   More fair the scenes appear.

The glowing tints of leaves and flowers,
The autumn blaze of trees and bowers,
   Glassed in the tranquil stream —
   How like a fairy dream!

MEMORIAL DAY.

GATHER flowers from cot and mansion,
  Gather flowers to deck the grave
Of our country's fallen heroes,
  " The unreturning brave."

Roses red and spotless lilies
  Strew upon their lowly bed,
Silent emblems of affection,
  Peaceful slumber of the dead !

Strew the fairest of May's offering
  Where the soldier-martyrs sleep ;
It will soothe the mourner's sorrow,
  Ever green their memory keep.

Come with banners; let sweet music
   Breathe her once-inspiring strain ;
Let the world know that the heroes
   Lying here fell not in vain.

For it was not lust for conquest
   Nor a cruel thirst for blood
Lured them on to meet the tempest,
   While it rained a deadly flood.

Well they loved the peaceful pathways
   Which their feet had trod so long ;
But they fought to save their country
   From Rebellion's traitorous throng.

Thus they stood before the nation,
   Grappling with her angry foes,
Knowing wounds, disease, and death are
   Not the worst of earthly woes.

All that was, by Heaven's favor,
　　Theirs to give they freely gave ;
And the death-blow that they welcomed
　　Broke the shackles of the slave.

Then bring flowers from cot and mansion,
　　Fairest flowers to deck the grave
Of our country's fallen heroes,
　　For they died this land to save.

THE OAK.

O'ERHEAD, among the branches tall,
    I heard a low wind sighing:
As if in answer to his call,
    The great oak spake, replying:

" Lofty above the grove I stand.
    A river past me flowing;
I smile to see the pleasant land,
    Where fruit and flowers are growing.

" Here, on a pleasant hillside, play
    Ye, summer winds, around me;
While centuries have rolled away,
    Just here you've always found me.

" I've seen the forests come and go,
    Shadow and sunlight sharing;
The slow decay, the axe-man's blow,
    And winter gale me sparing.

" Destroying wind, nor wasting rain,
    Nor frost-blight ever harms me;
The thunder shakes my form in vain,
    Its raging ne'er alarms me.

" I see below the waving corn
    And men, in distance calling;
Low-bending fields of grain at morn
    Before the reapers falling.

" And cottages for many a mile
    Dispersed, in sunlight glowing,
Where orchards smile through leafy aisle,
    And golden fruits are growing.

" My food ye, fickle winds, provide,
  Sweet dews the night wind shedding;
Kind earth bears nourishment beside
  To hungry roots far spreading.

" In turn my autumn leaves I shed.
  Food for the green herb yielding;
Dense leaves I now for shelter spread,
  From sun and tempest shielding.

" Here rests the toiler at noonday,
  In grateful shade reclining;
Here merry children come to play,
  Or lover sits repining.

" Here from the breathless mead the herd
  My tempting shade is bringing;
While in my arms the plaintive bird
  To weary day is singing.

4

" Here robin safely builds her nest,
  The topmost boughs selecting :
I screen her, in my arms at rest,
  With foliage protecting.

" I fling below the springing mast,
  In autumn branches folded,
And leaves by hand of autumn blast
  Gathered and o'er it moulded.

" I screen the young plants from the sun,
  From wind and tempest's raging ;
I scatter dews when day is done,
  Their summer thirst assuaging.

" And yet you see beneath my bough
  No healthy plant is springing,
But sickly reeds, that feebly grow,
  And flowers to frail stalk clinging.

" So fragile, whirled by autumn's gale,
　　They fly through field and alley
　Ere tender leaves around turn pale,
　　Exposed o'er hill and valley.

" And so it seems, my gentle breeze,
　　The plants we shield and cherish
　Grow weakly, living lives of ease,
　　And are the first to perish."

NED HAMMOND'S DREAM.

NED HAMMOND'S lonely cottage
　　Stood near a grassy plain,
One-storied, dark, unpainted,
　　And stained by sun and rain.

For ornament and finery
　　But little care had Ned;
For all new-fangled notions
　　He always had a dread.

He loved to tell quaint stories
　　And tales of former times,
When men, he claimed, were wiser,
　　Less common vice and crimes.

The scholar's gift and labor
    He flouted and despised :
But little else save farm-lore his
    Curriculum advised.

A neighbor roused his anger
    Who said the world was round,
That it forever wheeled and flew
    Through space.   'Twas also found

The sun and moon were worlds, too,
    Nor rose nor set at all,
Nor stars — worlds even greater, though
    They seemed so very small.

" Out on such pesky nonsense,"
    In anger, answered Ned ;
" Shall I not trust my senses nor
    Believe my eyes ?" he said.

It chanced one summer noonday
  Ned Hammond fell asleep ;
And while through open windows
  A breeze did softly creep

And fan his heated forehead,
  He had a wondrous dream.
He heard sweet music, faintly,
  Across a moonlit stream.

It might have been the breeze-song,
  Perchance a merry strain
Played on a harp, the fancy
  Waked in his sleeping brain.

But while he listened raptured,
  Before his dazzled sight
Grand Nature seemed in majesty
  To rise, revealed in light.

No longer veiled by distance, nor
    Appearing in disguise,
Each object its true image
    Revealed in earth and skies.

He saw the leaves, the pebbles,
    The flocks, and flashing rills
Where scarce before, dim-outlined,
    Appeared low, misty hills.

He saw the cloud-drawn shadows dance
    On far-off lakes and leas,
The gentle sphere-like curving
    Of land and distant seas.

Strange folk and far-off dwellings
    Greeted his wondering eyes;
But who shall tell the wonders
    That shone from unveiled skies?

The countless worlds and all therein —
  Such glory, light, and sheen,
Save in the dreams of fancy,
  Had mortal never seen.

All sounds to him were audible,
  For space confined no more.
The voice of wind and tempest,
  The ceaseless ocean roar,

The din of thousand cataracts
  And torrents far and near,
And myriad other voices
  And sounds surprised his ear.

At first the dreamer fearless saw
  The splendid scene unfold ;
'Twas but the harmless motion
  Of worlds, as he was told.

But now, when he gazed westward,
  He saw with sudden dread
The long horizon lifting
  Till, leaning o'er his head,

The hills upon him threatened
  Vast rocks and trees to throw:
The dizzy east sank downward
  Till yawned a gulf below.

He fell to earth, in terror
  The bare sod grasping, woke!
A fair world smiled upon him, not
  A sound the stillness broke.

Then truly he thanked Heaven
  So much in earth and sky
Had been withheld so wisely
  From man's weak ear and eye.

A MEMORY OF SCHOOL DAYS.[1]

THERE was a school-room — many a year
  Has perished since that day;
Along its walls was falling clear
  The winter sunset ray,

And glimmered in the dying flame
  The seats, in stately rows,
Where many a youth once sat whose fame
  A grateful country knows.

In front, a platform long and high;
  The teacher's desk was there,
Where long he sat with watchful eye,
  Sedate, with silvery hair.

Our task was ended, night was near,
　And one alone remained,
The teacher's calm reproof to hear
　For faulty work, detained.

That ended, on his glad ear fell
　These words of praise and cheer,
" But you are doing very well,"
　And " You must persevere."

Gone is the school-room where they met ;
　The faces, young and keen,
Of schoolmates dwell in memory yet,
　But nowhere else are seen.

Save that, 'mid busy scenes of life
　One now and then appears,
But changed in all by toil, by strife,
　By trace of wasting years.

And all are scattered, far and wide,
    Along the teeming West,
And near the bleak Atlantic's tide,
    While some have gone to rest.

No more the teacher's kindly word
    Cheers boyhood's toilful days:
No more on earth his voice is heard.
    Yet, in life's devious ways,

The student hears in every clime
    That gentle voice of cheer
Still echoing down the halls of time :
    " You must persevere."

As where the echoes on the Rhine
    Rebound from shore to shore,
May those who by its banks recline,
    Repeated o'er and o'er,

The words they utter plainly hear
  Echoed from every hill,
So to his mind these words of cheer
  Come oft returning still.

And so, in turn, some heart to cheer,
  Lost hope, perchance, reclaim,
And scatter seeds may ripen here
  In deeds of worthy fame,

Now, after many weary days,
  These words he would repeat ;
And say to all life's thorny ways
  Pursue with weary feet :

To all who battle for the right
  Yet pause in doubt and fear,
Through ways of darkness, ways of light :
  Forever persevere.

THE WRECK OF THE SEA BIRD.

[Wrecked on the coast of Long Island during the storm of
January 9th, 1886.]

THE wind swept landward, angry and cold :
   In from the sea the great waves rolled :
Hurrying storm clouds, low and dun,
Stretched their shadows beneath the sun.

Down came the snows, an icy swarm,
Till nothing was seen but the blinding storm :
Right in the eyes of the sailors flew,
Hiding the decks and the waters blue.

Strong ships lay broken on strand and rock,
Wrecked that day by the tempest shock.
Yet one brave schooner, through storm and spray,
Held for a time her perilous way.

'Mid the dreadful din, the rushing blast
Tossed the spray over rigging and mast,
Lifted the billows that thundering rose
Above the vessel: like wanton foes

They clutched at the yards, the sails, and the men,
Bore off the boat and the hatches, and then
Leapt on the deck and pounded the side,
Till through the wide seams they let in the tide.

In vain, the merciless gale to flee,
The heavy cargo is flung to the sea ;
No human hand the vessel may guide.
Vainly anchors are cast from her side.

For the chains soon part, and, helpless, to shore
The vessel drifts amid the roar,
Where captain and sailors, half-frozen, half-dead,
Lie waiting the death they scarcely dread.

Over all the coast the wrecks are strown :
Round them the wild winds shriek and moan.
Mourn, sad winds, for the wrecked and the lost,
On the surf-beat rocks and beaches tossed,

Frozen and drowned on the terrible day :
Stretched on the icy strand they lay.
Now on a cold and desolate shore,
Good Farmer Corwin, marking the roar,

Sees, beyond the dreadful rote,
Something still on the waves afloat.
" Bring my glass," the farmer said.
He looked far out where the waters spread ;

Then launched his boat, and rapidly rowed
Out on the deep, where a signal showed
Some one in peril upon the tide,
Till he reached the stranded schooner's side.

All was still but the waves and the gale :
Stiff and moveless the ice-covered sail ;
Forsaken the deck ; not a sound within
Mingled with ocean's ceaseless din.

But down in the cabin, dank and old,
Five men were lying and dying with cold.
Rouse, dying sailors, one comes to save
You all from death and an ocean grave.

Kind hearts, too, wait in a cot on the shore
To welcome you back to land once more.
Strong hands now clasp each sturdy form,
And bear from the cabin drenched by the storm,

In safety, over wave and foam.
All back to the joys of a cheerful home.
"God bless the farmer ! " the sailors said :
And many more who the story read.

A GERMAN STORY.

A BROOK, to whose green margin
    The smiles of May brought cheer,
For ages long had fed the glades
    And boughs that blossomed near,

Not oft by floods annoying,
    Since rugged banks restrained.
One morning came a shepherd,
    Who mournfully complained

Because a mighty river,
    That in a verdant plain
Lay coiling like a serpent,
    A petted lamb had slain.

The brook attentive listened, then
Indignantly replied :
" O cruel river, flowing
Through valley fair and wide.

" If thy dark, turbid waters
Were only clear as mine,
What ghastly sights would be revealed,
What dole 'neath waves that shine !

" Were I a mighty river
In valley fair and wide,
By blooming forests shaded,
Rich meadows by my side,

" No living creature would I harm,
But all would aid and cheer ;
Nor for the safety of his flock
Should worthy shepherd fear."

There came a fearful tempest
　Ere many suns had passed ;
The brook, its vale o'erflowing, grew
　A torrent loud and fast.

Through meadow, park, and forest
　It dashed, it foamed, it poured,
O'er ruined lawn and garden :
　Down to the sea it roared.

And on its heaving bosom
　Huge branches floated down,
Fair dwellings, crushed and broken,
　The wrecks of deluged town.

Amid the din and tumult,
　Ere closed the dreadful day,
The shepherd, and his cottage.
　And flocks were swept away.

So many a brook sings gaily,
　And, cheering glade and bower,
It dashes on, and nothing harms
　Because it lacks the power.

THE THIEF AND THE QUAKER.

ONE summer morn, 'mid shade and bloom
 A country farm-house stood;
The farmer, dozing in his room,
 Seemed in unhappy mood;
Kind fortune gave an ample store,
But, like most men, he wanted more.

Just now had failed his wheat supply;
 'Tis true that wheat was cheap,
And he had money, too, to buy,
 But that he wished to keep;
And so contrived this foolish man,
To save his cash, a wicked plan.

One stormy night, when none could see,
   Donning his cloak and hat,
He sought a Quaker's granary,
   And filled his own from that.
Emboldened by success, again
He went to steal his neighbor's grain.

But now. though night would veil the deed,
   'Twas marked by one keen eye ;
The Quaker saw how shrank his seed,
   Perhaps suspected why ;
And thief, not half his journey through,
Heard steps behind that nearer drew.

" Thee has a heavy burden, friend,"
   The Quaker kindly said ;
" Thee must be weary, let me lend
   A hand." As on they sped,
So hard he urged, the man at last
Gave up his burden ; on they passed.

They reached a farm-house ; in a bin
  The stolen wheat they poured ;
And then, the farmer's cot within,
  They, sitting by the board
As oft before, engaged in chat
About their crops, and this and that.

At last, when late the hour was found,
  The Quaker sought the door,
But, ere he went, he turned around —
  His neighbor thought before
He spoke he was about to say,
"Good night to thee," then go away.

Instead of that: "My friend, that wheat —
  It is so nearly gone,
I cannot spare thee more of it
  Before my crop comes on."
Up sprang the farmer from his seat ;
He seized his purse :   "O, yes, that wheat !

"That wheat ! I'll pay you for that wheat !"
"O, never mind it, friend ;
I think we have enough to eat,
But none to sell nor lend."
"Say double, triple, what you will,
Here, take it ; only keep it still."

"I could n't, neighbor, if I would,
It is no use to try :
I could n't keep it, it's too good ;
I'd only tell a lie."
Then, all unmindful of his grief,
The Quaker left the frantic thief.

Whether they live or now are dead
The muse inquired in vain ;
Of thief, it hardly need be said,
He never stole again.
The moral — if it need be told :
Better to speak kind words than scold.

WINTERGREEN.

A^N April wind sighed, as it passed,
   A long sigh of relief,
As one who rests from labor vast,
   Or after vanished grief.

Beside a river, near concealed
   Beneath a moss-made screen,
Thin woods around and rocky field,
   Are leaves of wintergreen.

Three bright, red berries, plump and round,
   One thread-like stem sustains;
They grow upon a lowly mound,
   Fed by the winter rains.

The frost king builds his palace cold
  On frozen streamlet near;
The snows this little plant enfold,
  The winds blow chill and drear.

All winter its lone task it plied,
  Deprived of light and sun;
E'en rivalling the summer's pride
  Its work, when it was done.

Cold mire below, or frosty ground,
  The gales did o'er it swell;
The savory atom still it found
  To build the tiny cell.

The cells it bound, and gave them form,
  In bright and glossy rind.
Unseen, it wrought through calm and storm.
  A chemist rare to find,

Whose cunning hand, without display,
 Can fashion thus at will
Such forms from shapeless, lifeless clay —
 Surpassing human skill.

Out of materials crude and cold
 Not even Liebig's art
Could growing fruit like this unfold,
 Nor could he life impart.

MORNING.

" Fighting for light and the freedom it brings."
— *James A. Garfield.*

L IGHT and the freedom which it brings
Are still the goal toward which life tends.
High in the east the morning sends
Arrows of light with golden wings:
Grim night and darkness steal away
Before the march of conquering day.

Now are we free to roam the field ;
If aught our doubtful step misleads,
Or mound, or dike, or stone impedes,
All in the brightness are revealed,
While every object glows in light
That rose so phantom-like by night.

So night and darkness flee before
 The beaming light which knowledge sheds,
 And where were gloom and chaos, spreads
A scene delightful evermore :
And free through all the glowing space
New worlds of thought and bliss we trace.

SHADOWS.

IN the dusk of maple shadows
  A lowly cottage stands;
Upon the moss-grown window sill
  Are prints of tiny hands.

Across its well-worn threshold,
  Beside which blooms the rose,
One passed who never has returned.
  Where struggled valiant foes

On rebel fields his steps were led:
  But where and how he fell,
By wound, disease, in prison,
  No tongue nor tidings tell.

And now a shadow, deeper
　　Than densest branches throw
Upon the moss-grown cottage roof,
　　Falls on the rooms below.

To manhood and to womanhood
　　The children all have grown ;
A mother gray, bereft of all,
　　Sits in her room alone.

The shadows, never lifting, while
　　The years are rolling on.
In saddened heart still lingers in
　　The cottage by the lawn.

THE BEST OFTEN LIES NEAREST.

WHERE the woodland branches twine,
　　With the breeze its leaves at play,
Is a single fruitful vine,
　　Bent across the narrow way.

Dark and ripe the clusters linger,
　　Ready for the tempted hand,
And with long and briery finger
　　Seize me, and my way command.

But in vain they seek protection
　　From the birds that hover there;
Haply, mindful of perfection,
　　They would choose some matron's care.

6

Fain would deck her table light ;
   As the stars through vapors beam,
Placidly in dishes white
   They would smile through clouds of cream.

Wandered had I, long in vain,
   Through the forest far and near,
Gathering all with toil and pain,
   Berries poorer than are here.

After many a thorn-made wound,
   After journey of an hour
To and fro, at last I found,
   Luckily, all I sought and more.

So, methinks, it is ofttimes,
   What we long seek far away,
Seek perchance in foreign climes,
   After toiling and delay,

Be it happiness or pleasure.

Be it wealth or other store,

We at last the long-sought treasure

Find, it may be, at our door.

EVENING IN AUTUMN.

A GROUP of circling hills that tower,
  Wood-crowned or bare, o'er vale and sea,
 Where shadows, pointing eastwardly,
Grow longer, longer every hour.
Till, crossed at length the cool, dark glades,
They blend with eve's returning shades.

Light clouds in purple lines, at rest,
  Like ships upon a sea of gold
  That fair and breezeless skies enfold,
At anchor lie far in the west;
And on the farthest hills below,
Fire-tipped and still, the forests glow.

Deep in the forest, where a stream,
 Unruffled, glasses sky and shore
 And noiselessly deep waters pour,
Bright tints of autumn foliage gleam ;
While not a leaf nor wave is stirred,
Nor sound of busy life is heard.

FINALE.

I STAND in the gray October
  By a river still and cold ;
I mark the gleaming foliage.
  The crimson, green, and gold,
Beneath the placid waters.
  In the mirror of a stream,
While below the dazzling sunbeams
  Through branches upward gleam.

I behold a sky unclouded
  Far beneath the river's bed,
Serene, like the dome of azure
  Bending silently o'erhead.

On the marge a spring-wove carpet
  Lies, stained by frozen dews ;
One aster blossom mingles
  Its light with darker hues.

Here and there, along the valley,
  Lessening shadows circle 'round
Wide-spreading elms and maples,
  Whose foliage strews the ground.
A bird to the rocky margin
  Now comes with the waves to play :
In the cold stream bathes her plumage,
  Then silently soars away.

Above in the leaves a rustle,
  A flutter, but never a song,
Where flit two lonely sparrows,
  The last of summer's throng.
It is sad in the golden harvest time
  To mark the swift decay

That has darkened the summer landscape,
    As night overshadows the day.

But we know in the heart of Nature
    The warm life-blood still flows ;
Not death means this deep stillness,
    But rest and a brief repose.
Only rest from toiling and striving
    That are soon to be renewed,
From growing, and fruit-bearing,
    And the endless search for food.

With the music of breeze, and woodland,
    And streamlet she will rise,
With the bloom and verdure of spring-time
    And the glow of summer skies.
As her children wake from slumber
    Which darksome night has blessed,
As the soul from death's deep silence,
    She will wake from her wintry rest.

These banks and fields will again be green,
  The hills be clothed anew ;
These branches ring with bird-song,
  And sparkle with morning dew.
Thanks, Nature, for the lesson
  Thou teachest everywhere :
In dread decay and ruin is,
  Not death, but rest from care.

EARLY PIECES.

SNOW-FLAKES.

THE clouds were slowly sailing past
    One stormy autumn day,
And snow-flakes, falling thick and fast,
    On mead and forest lay.

On roof and lawn, the leafless rose,
    And whitened street they pour:
But when again the morning glows
    The snows are seen no more.

And now no vestige, name, or date
    Of lives so transient tell ;
Yet in this record read the fate
    Of human lives as well.

And yet the snows that from the light
    Have vanished for a while,
Though mixed with clay, will, pure and bright,
    Again in fountain smile.

Again will seek their first long home
    And dwell in deep, wide sea ;
And thus a type their lives become
    Of immortality.

IN MEMORY.

w. w.

FRIEND of my boyhood,[5] thou didst guide
  To nobler paths my wayward feet ;
Thy hand the portal opened wide
  That led to Learning's fair retreat.
No more thy pleasant face we see,
  Thy kindly voice no longer hear :
O many hearts will grieve for thee,
  And long will miss thy presence dear.

Twice summer's blushing flowers have come,
  Her zephyrs passed thee with a sigh,
And now around thy silent home
  The withered leaves of autumn lie.

Now sorrow ceases to relate
 Thy story as before ; in sleep
She dreams of thee and thy hard fate.
 Or wakes, in solitude to weep.

'Twas not for me to note the slow
 Decline, while luring hope in vain
Endured ; to joy when slumber low
 One moment loosed the grasp of pain :
To watch by thee while more and more
 The shadows round thee darkly creep.
But now thy journey brief is o'er,
 Thy work is done. and thou dost sleep.

Yet, as a lone star in the night
 Its lustre sheds 'mid parting clouds,
While others shine with fainter light
 Or hide beneath their misty shrouds.

Or as a river, broad and bright,

   Cleaving the dusky vale appears,

E'en so thy memory's tender light

   Shines through the sorrow-darkened years.

THE DRUNKARD'S MISTAKE.

ONE bitter cold and blustering night,
　　When loud the wild winds blew,
A tavern door-way, open wide,
　　A drunkard staggered through;
Scarce wit had he to find the street
Or power his frightened nag to beat.

A man he was once well-to-do,
　　But now, like many more,
Not what he was or might have been,
　　By drunkenness made poor.
The scene through which his journey led
Had learned his noisy brawls to dread.

With shouts and curses, when he passed,
  The peaceful valley rang,
With shriek and yell and sometimes song,
  Whip-stroke and sleigh-bells' clang.
The startled country people near
Know well the drunken voice they hear.

And did no ill this rum-crazed man
  Afflict with grief or pain?
Ah, yes, not half, if all were told,
  This volume would contain.
Pray, list, and I will briefly tell
What next that dreary night befell.

As on he sped the landscape drear
  And eastern sky grew light;
And soon upon a low hill near
  A cheerful fire shone bright.
Soon as his dull eyes chanced to spy it,
He paused, and sought to warm him by it.

7

Through drifts he staggered till a screen
   Opposed, both strong and high ;
He bared his feet, and, sitting down,
   He raised them up to dry,
Thinking to warm them in the blaze
Behind the screen, that met his gaze.

It chanced a traveller that night,
   This lone way forced to go,
A team found standing in the road,
   A voice heard in the snow,
'Mid curses, screaming words like these :
" Pile on more wood ! I shall (hic) freeze !"

There by the road the drunkard lay,
   As crazy as a loon ;
His aching feet thrust through a fence,
   And warming by the moon.
Kind reader, if you'd not surpass
Such fools in folly, shun the glass !

MEMORIES.

WHEN we retrace, in thoughtful mien,
  Some pleasant pathway long forsaken,
Behold again a well-known scene
Where childhood passed, or youth serene,
  What long-forgotten memories waken !

E'en so this quiet autumn day,
  While through these once familiar groves
I wander, not yet far away,
The dim Past rises from decay,
  And notes the fading hours it loves.

'Tis sad, indeed, to mark the glow
  Of silent hills that give no breath,
The wan leaves on the moveless bough,
The gray fields, verdureless, below
  Fair Nature's calm repose in death.

Yet in this lifeless view I've read
  A record long of pleasant dreams ;
Like a vast tome, with leaves outspread ; —
When oped by Morn with fingers red,
  I scanned its pages by their gleams.

I mark the scenes that come and go ;
  This rustling screen of branches past,
I see the gleaming waters flow,
As through the gloomy present show
  Fond memories that gather fast.

I hear the tap of lightsome wave ;
   They beat the heaving prow no more ;
I see the gloom of darksome cave
On steep and rugged hill that gave
   The wavering shadows by the shore.

Then there are haunts in open field,
   Where on some height the wild vines creep,
Where solitary oak may shield
Or hardy fruit tree that may yield
   Some fruit, despite the windy steep.

And through the veil of grove and lawn,
   Of waters bright and branches sere,
I view the scenes of life's bright dawn,
The forms of dear ones who have gone,
   And never, save in dreams, appear.

NOTES.

NOTE 1, p. 22.

" *A worthy man.*"

Rev. Enos George, who was settled as pastor of the Con-
gregational Church in Barnstead, N. H., in 1803, and continued
in the ministry in that town for more than fifty-five years.
" His rank as a pulpit orator was high, his manners dignified,
and his sermons models of system, Scriptural allusion, and
good language." — *Biographical sketch.*

NOTE 2, p. 39.

" *The Suncook bears its ancient name.*"

Owing to the fact that the Indians had forsaken this region
before the white settlers arrived, no Indian name, with the
exception of the Suncook, either of hill, plain, or stream, has
been preserved.

NOTE 3, p. 43.

" Few vestiges to trace."

Tribes of Pennacook Indians formerly occupied the valley of the Suncook. Indian weapons and utensils have been occasionally discovered near the river.

NOTE 4, p. 58.

The incident here related occurred many years ago at Phillips Academy, Exeter, N. II., while Dr. G. L. Soule was principal.

NOTE 5, p. 93.

" Friend of my boyhood."

William Walker, M. D., to whom the author was greatly indebted for assistance and encouragement in obtaining an education.